never got over you

WILLOW WINTERS

Copyright © 2023, Willow Winters Publishing.

All rights reserved. willowwinterswrites.com

No part of this publication may be reproduced, stored in a retrieval system, or transmitted in any form or by any means, electronic, mechanical, photocopying, recording, scanning, or otherwise, without the prior written permission of the publisher, except in the case of brief quotations within critical reviews and otherwise as permitted by copyright law.

NOTE: This is a work of fiction.

Names, characters, places, and incidents are a product of the author's imagination.

Any resemblance to real life is purely coincidental. All characters in this story are 18 or older.

never got over you

Prologue

Bennet

The wheels on the creeper board add a hum to the asphalt as I roll out from under the car at the sound of her heels clicking. Dirty blonde hair frames her gorgeous face as she bites down on the bottom of her lip. On my back where I am, with the light in my eyes, I swear to God she looks like a fucking angel on earth. The worn down blue jeans hug her curvy hips and the tank top she's wearing shows just a touch of cleavage.

"What are you doing here?" I question, not able to keep the grin from showing. My heart beats faster, wilder as she crouches down and I know just what she's going to do.

"I just missed you," she tells me. Her eyes shine with a look that I love. It's a tempting one with hope and something else. I think she loves me. Although that would be too good to be true.

I'm instantly hard as she straddles me. "You're a tease, Bree," I groan.

With a sweet feminine laugh she flips her hair to the side and leans down to kiss me. Both of my hands move to her hips and I help her get comfortable.

I peek up at the clock on the wall, and lick my lower lip, eager to take advantage of the privacy I'm almost sure we have.

The garage is empty, everyone else is most certainly gone for the night since it's 6. I'm the only mechanic still here, and this car can wait.

Everything can wait for her. That's the only truth I know anymore.

She squeals with laughter as I roll us down a good bit and she's free to lean forward.

"I got you," I tell her as her palms fall down on my chest. Fuck. She looks too damn good like this.

Smelling like honey with her hair tickling down my neck.

I'm sure I smell like oil and sweat, working out here all day. But my Bree doesn't mind getting a little dirty.

I rock her back and forth on the creeper, loving how she lays down on top of me.

"You're so bad."

"You're the one who came here after hours …" I tease her.

With every little movement I kiss her. It's short and sweet and she tucks her hair behind her ear, settling down and getting comfortable.

I love it.

Just then the sky darkens a touch behind us, letting the moonlight come through and the crisp night air is felt with a gust of wind.

She deepens the kiss and I know I'm done for. This woman has all of me.

Bree hooks her leg around mine and I stop the roller. "You know exactly why I came," she murmurs against my lips. Her soft curves are warm against me and everything about this is a dream come true.

"Cause you're in love with me?" I ask her and once

again my heart does an odd skip and then races like it's far too excited.

"Madly and deeply," she responds like it's a joke. Like she doesn't quite mean it.

There's a spark there though when I lean down and kiss her again and she's the one to deepen it. She's the one who pushes for more.

She loves me. I fucking know she does.

And I love her too. One day I'll tell her. Maybe one day soon.

chapter One

Aubrey

Three weeks earlier

"You're my hero," I tell Lauren as I slip out of her car.

"Anytime. Have a good day babe," she answers easily. My neighbor and good friend is going to be a bit late to work so she could drop me off, and I appreciate it.

The passenger side car door closes with a heavy clunk and I wave goodbye as she drives off. A chilly early spring breeze graces my shoulders and blows back my hair as I turn to face the garage. I can already smell the oil and the clanking and drilling are easily heard.

Joe's shop is on the edge of town and there's nothing much around but woods and dirt. He used to have a place on main street, with all the quaint shops and corner stores, but he outgrew it.

My heels sit in the dirt and I second guess wearing my navy shift dress to pick up my car.

Car, coffee, meeting with my boss at two, and then drinks with the girls at six. I check my watch as I mentally go over my to do list. I have plenty of time. It's not every day the director of publication comes to town but she insisted we have a sit down and a drink to celebrate my promotion to chief editor. The little bits of happiness stir in the pit of my stomach as I open the shop door and bells chime above my head.

Life is good. Dream house on Cedar Lane, dream job with a pay increase to boot, great friends ... just missing one little thing. Someone to love and share it with.

Lauren reminded me of that on the ride over.

Technically Lauren tried to change drink with the

girls, to drinks out on the town... I'm not so sure I'm wanting to though.

It's been years since I've been on a date. Work simply got ahead of me. Even as I stand at the front desk, waiting on someone to come up so I can get my keys and head out, I feel butterflies at the thought of dating.

Joe, with his scruff and oil stained blue overalls comes around the corner.

"Morning Aubrey," he greets me with a grin and grabs my keys from the pin board before coming up to the register.

"Good morning," I answer him and ask him how his wife is doing. Small talk is easy in a small town. As he rings me up, I rock on my heels and laugh with him about the school board meeting last week. I don't have kids and I don't have any reason to know what happened apart from the fact that gossip always gets around town.

"And thank you for being so fast with my car."

"We have more help now so it's not a problem."

"Oh," I respond, not realizing he hired anyone. "That's wonderful. Business must be booming."

"That it is," he nods and then tells me I'm all set and to make my way out back.

With an easy goodbye, I head down the hall to take a shortcut to the back, and that's when I see him.

Those butterflies stir up faster and I swear time slows as Bennet wipes his hands down with a blue washcloth already marred with oil. My heart pitter patters as I inhale and attempt to remember who I am and what I'm doing.

His eyes lift and lock with mine and I'm caught, staring at my highschool crush who's all grown up. His broad shoulders make the dirty white tee stretch tight and his forearms are corded with muscle I'll never be able to unsee.

"Bennet," I barely get out his name before letting out a scream as I nearly topple over something hard. Ouch! I reach out to catch myself and my hands land on his hard chest. Instantly warmth and a masculine scent surround me.

Holy shit.

"You alright?" Bennet asks, righting me. His hands are like fire on mine. Tension is thick and I feel foolish. My cheeks burn with a blush and I swallow down my highschool memories.

"Fine, fine," I breathe out and take half a step back to give him space. "Thank you," I whisper as

I'm caught in his pale blue gaze again. His asymmetric simper is everything. His rough stubble and a charming smile makes me weak in the knees.

How the hell is he even hotter than I remember?

"Sorry," I apologize and he holds his palms up and out, "You're fine, Bree."

Bree. Oh my goodness it's been years since anyone has called me that. It's never sounded better than from him though.

"Didn't know you were back in town," I comment and instantly my gaze drops down as he licks his lower lip.

Hot and bothered is an understatement. I had no idea that a mechanic was a fantasy of mine until I set my sights on him.

I clear my throat, gripping my keys and purse and attempting to gather composure. I'm so embarrassed.

Bennet seems as unphased as ever, "Got in last week," he tells me. Nodding, I realize I'm lost in thought and desperately try to shake off the puppy dog love that's come over me.

"Sorry I was just," I point past him to the

parking lot. "My car," I attempt to explain. My cheeks growing hotter by the second.

"Let me help you," he offers out a hand and I step forward, my heel slips on not a darn thing, I slip forward and his hand brushes my breast.

"Sorry."

"Sorry!"

We apologize for the awkward encounter in unison and my heart beats so fast out of sheer embarrassment. What the hell is wrong with me?

"I, uh, didn't mean,"

"It's fine, it's fine," I wave his concern away, fix my dress with a quick tug and lead the way to the parking lot so I can escape. "I've got it," I assure him and he makes no attempt to follow although I can feel his eyes on me.

"Good to see you," I offer as I come to the end of the garage and turn to give him a wave, nearly tripping again. These heels are my arch nemesis after this encounter. Never again.

"You alright?" he calls out and I offer a lined, tight smile as I answer, "I'm fine."

My heart is still racing as I climb into my car and slip the keys into the ignition. What the hell was that? I wish the earth would open up and swallow me whole.

As I'm sitting my purse in the passenger seat, my mind still racing with embarrassment, there's a knock on my window that catches me off guard.

I roll it down all the while trapped in that gorgeous blue gaze. At least my butt is in the seat so I can't fall over anything. Surely, I'm head over heels for this man.

"Yes?" I ask as he sheepishly looks down at me, that blue washcloth still in his hands and this time being rung by them.

"You want to … maybe get lunch?" He swallows thickly and I've never known how sexy an adam's apple can be.

"I have a business thing," I admit at the same time that I'm trying to process whether or not Bennet Thompson has just asked me out. "Do you want to get dinner?" I offer without thinking

"Dinner.. How very forward of you," he teases with a charming grin and instantly the tension relaxes. I can only blink away my disbelief before he answers, "I'd love to."

Love … that's a word. That's a word for Bennet Thomspon.

"I'll get your number from Joe and text you?" he offers and I nod, "Yeah that sounds good."

He pats the hood of my car once. "See you tonight," he tells me. "Drive safer than you walk Bree," he jokes and smiles at me in a way that has a wanting need making everything in my car hotter than it should be.

chapter Two

Bennet

Aubrey Peters. I can't believe she's still in this town ... and single. When Joe told me she was coming to pick up her car... Well, I haven't felt nervousness like that since I was a kid.

Never in my wildest dreams did I think I'd ever see her again let alone take her out on the town.

I have to admit I thought about her when I told my family I was coming home. The heat around my collar grows so I tug it gently before climbing out of the truck.

Joe lent me the old beat up Ford and it's at odds with my attire. Not that my slacks and a crisp button down with rolled up sleeves is fancy, the truck is just more on the rustic side. I'm grateful for it though. I sold my car before moving and I'm still waiting on everything that was shipped to arrive. I look over my shoulder at the truck and hope Aubrey doesn't think I'm broke. Afterall, I'm crashing at a friend's and borrowing a truck that looks like it doesn't belong on Cedar Lane.

Everything is just a week delayed and it's all a mess.

Unlike her perfectly manicured lawn and the picture book Craftsman house with a painted blue door.

I'm not surprised Aubrey made a life for herself like this. We were neighbors growing up and even though I was a bit older, we were friends enough that I knew her well.

I knew her hopes and dreams and knew her family and what they thought of mine. A girl like her was never going to date a guy like me. Even now I know she's too good for me, but I couldn't not take the chance. With the way she looked at me, with how much I missed her... shaking out my hands, I try not to remind myself that tonight has to go perfect. I already know that's what a woman like Aubrey deserves.

I swallow thickly before knocking. My nerves are a damn mess but they're quickly subdued. Bree opens the door within seconds. She must've been waiting for me.

"You look beautiful," I tell her without thinking twice.

"Same dress as this morning," she says shyly as she steps out.

I grin down at her, she's so much shorter. "Like I said, beautiful." A beautiful blush flushes all the way from her chest to her temple and I remember just how shy Bree was back in school. She surprises me though with a compliment of my own, "You look good yourself," she says.

As if my pulse couldn't get any faster. Hell, I think my own cheeks may be a hue of red as I slip my arm around her waist and guide her to the truck. "This is our ride for the night."

She doesn't seem put off in the least as I open the door and help her up.

"Just borrowing this one," I tell her as if it's an excuse.

"I'm not judging. It'll run better than my car did last week," she jokes and it eases my worry.

It's not until I'm on my side and turning the ignition over that I tell her where we're going.

The idle rumble of the truck rides with us as we drive downtown through so many places I remember as a kid. "Town looks almost the same," I comment.

"Did you hear that Steve bought the bar?"

Nodding, I tell her I did, "Joe told me. He's filling me in on some things," I tell her as I slow down at a stop sign and glance to my right. She's a beautiful sight. Perched on the seat in her blue dress and looking up at me through thick lashes.

"He filled you in on me?" she asks and I only nod, feeling my throat go tight.

"What'd he tell you? I always wonder what this town has to say about me," she asks almost teasingly.

"Not much to be fair," I answer her. "Just that you're a hot shot with some publishing company in New York."

She scoffs, "I wouldn't say hot shot. Just an editor."

never got over *you*

"Just an editor," I arch a brow. "Isn't that what you always wanted?"

Her smile brightens and lights up her face. Fuck, adrenaline runs through me as I'm brought back to that same look she had when we were just kids. "Yeah, I got my dream job," she admits.

"I'm happy for you," I tell her and mean it and she plays it off with a joke.

It's almost like old times. Easy, carefree, like the two of us are just keeping each other company as we grow up in a small town with not much to do but throw rocks in the creek and watch drive in movies.

The conversation flows easily, although the tension is still there. Thick and hot.

"When did you get back?"

"Couple days ago. Joe needed someone to help with the garage."

"You guys stayed close when you moved away?"

"Yeah," I admit to her. "He came down to visit a few times too." I went to college out of state then traveled a bit doing odds and ends. Anything to keep my mind off this town and how much I both loved and hated it. Loved the people in it. Hated how I felt trapped there as a kid.

"So you came to help out?" she asks.

"Yeah, I did always like working on cars," I tell her and my palms are so sweaty they slip a bit on the leather steering wheel. When I come to a stop at the red light just before the steak house, I wipe them off on my slacks and hope she can't tell just how nervous I am. "I loved the west coast but I'm happy to be home. Been missing it, you know?" I say and our eyes catch.

"Yeah I can see that," she says looking at me with a beautiful simper and a look in her eyes I can't place.

As we park in the side lot to the restaurant, the air shifts between us. "What happened with us?" she asks me in a tone that holds too much emotion.

"What do you mean?" I ask her even though I know exactly what she means. We were close until we weren't. She was a good friend until I felt more and knew what I wanted could never be.

"When you left town, I never heard from you."

"We weren't that close in the last years of high school," I tell her, knowing exactly why that happened.

"Did I do something back then?" she asks me and my heart races.

"Not at all. Why would you think that?" I ask,

never got over *you*

turning off the truck. She fiddles with the seatbelt, before saying never mind and that she's just in her head. She laughs it off and I do too. As if I don't know that I'm the one who ruined it. I'm the one who put that distance between us.

As I shut my door and make my way around to hers, I pray like hell that she realizes I want more than to just be friends. I think she does too. I fucking hope she does.

chapter
Three

Aubrey

I'M NOT THE ONLY ONE WHO DIDN'T KNOW Bennet was back in town.

That's the way it is in a small town. A few patrons stop him to give a wave and a former teacher, and the football coach, stands to give him a quick pat on the back. The smiles on their faces are genuine.

The waiter comes, a college aged gentleman I don't recognize with slick back hair and a crisp white top. He holds a pad of paper in one hand with the pen balanced with his thumb as he pours our water and then explains the specials. I've been to Timothy's a handful of times, mostly with the girls. It's a nice place to celebrate anniversaries and birthdays, fancy dinners and such.

And I suppose first dates with highschool crushes who have come back home.

I keep glancing up at Bennet, fiddling with my menu, and wondering what I've missed from his life.

The moment we're alone my phone pings and pings again and I reach into my purse to silence it and to also respond to the group chat that I will update them after. I assumed it would mostly be "good luck" messages but a quick peek proves Lauren and Marlena are debating the odds of this date ending with a kiss.

Heat rises up my chest and I'm quick to shove the phone into my purse.

It's been years since I've talked to Bennet. But not years since I've thought back on the feelings I had for him.

"Everything okay?" he asks as I set my purse strap down over the back of the chair and I answer of course, but my throat is drier than I expected.

Can I not catch a break?

never got over *you*

"I'm not usually this—" I almost say clumsy but I think I mean nervous. Either way before I can finish, Bennet finishes the sentence for me, "squeaky?"

His smirk isn't hidden behind the glass as he lifts it to his lips and I have to laugh.

I'm saved by the waiter and we both place our orders. A cajun pasta with blackened shrimp for him and a tuscan chicken dish that looks delish for me.

It turns quiet for only a moment as I drink down my nerves. Thankfully Bennet changes the subject.

"Haven't been here in years," Bennet says and I take a quick peek around. We're in a booth in the far corner of the back room. It's more private, the conversation more muted from the front room where the bar is, the lights are even dimmer. "Still looks the same though."

"White table cloths with tea lights and cloth napkins is pretty much a staple," I respond and almost say it's perfect for a first date. My lips part and I nearly ask him, is this just a friendly meal or is there a possibility for something more? Almost, but I don't.

I already decided when I was chatting with the girls earlier and filling them in on how I became Humpty Dumpty in the garage that I would treat it like a date, whether or not he is. Afterall, there may only be friendship between us. All of those butterflies and emotions could be built up from years of memories.

"Perfect for a first date," Bennet says and as my eyes swoop up to his, he looks past me and takes a sip of his draft beer.

"Don't you think?" he adds when he finally looks back at me.

"I do," I answer and then shake off the lust filled tone and clear my throat, opting for water over my wine.

The flutter in my chest picks up and my smile comes easier. As does the conversation. It flows as easily as the drinks. The night is filled with good food and easy conversation. Within the hour, our forks are scraping against the plates for the last bits of deliciousness and my cheeks are sore from smiling so much.

"So that's why you moved out there? To help Grant with his bar?"

"Yeah, that and I had a little business for a minute, a start up but I sold it."

"Oh I saw that. You did well with it, didn't you?"

"You saw… of course you did, it's such a small town."

"I admit, I occasionally saw a social media post here and there too,"

He nods, a smirk on his face. "Since we're admitting things, I'll admit I asked Joe about you. He didn't just volunteer that information."

"Oh you were asking about me?" My voice is a little too peppy, and I'm quick to take another sip.

His fingers slide up his beer glass and I find myself drawn to the movement. Wondering what all those fingers are going to do tonight.

"I don't want you thinking I'm not on my feet just because I'm helping out at the shop and crashing on a friend's couch."

"I didn't think much of it. You've always known what you were doing and made it work," I tell him and it's true. Benent was always helping everyone else. The fact that that's what he did with his life, following friends and helping them with their dreams while building his businesses on the side just seems to fit with the version of him I knew.

"Do you regret it?" I ask him.

"Nah," he answers quickly and then he seems to second guess it as our eyes lock. The tension turns hotter and desire stirs between my legs. He clears his throat and then tells me, "I mean, I regret leaving some people. I regret how much time passed. But I'm happy to be home," he tells me.

Some people. I wonder if it would be presumptuous to think I might be one of them. I always felt something between us. I debate on telling him that I had a thing for him. That I was heartbroken when he left. But he does it again. He beats me to the punch.

"Back then, I always had a thing for you. Had to get out of town before I could ask and you turn me down."

"You're kidding," the surprise is evident in my tone. "Why didn't you ever say?"

"You were younger, your family was a bit more strict… I figured it was a no before I even asked."

"That's a shame cause I always had a thing for you too."

Bennet's charming smile does something devilish to me. Something sinister with desire. "I um, I probably should have asked before," I gather up the courage to say. "You don't have a girlfriend do you?"

"Not at all. Actually I was hoping if you had a good time tonight, you might want to do it again?"

"Do it again.. As in tonight is over?" I gather my phone to see two things. The first is that it's nearly ten and four hours have passed. The second is that my friends are making bets and joking that the odds are now favoring a sleepover more than just a good night kiss. Just reading it forces a heat through me.

"I mean… we could always …" Bennet starts and I gather up the courage to go for it. There's nothing like the present moment to go for something I thought would never happen.

"Want to come back to my place?" I offer and Bennet's expression flashes shock and then it darkens.

"You don't waste any time do you?" Bennet asks and then waves the waiter for the check.

I only blush violently and I don't say it out loud, but I think more than enough time has passed.

chapter Four

Bennet

THE DRIVE WAS FAR TOO LONG AND FAR too quiet for Bree to keep her hands to herself.

It started easy enough with me placing a hand on her thigh. Her weaving her fingers through mine. And then she took it upon herself to slip the tip of my finger up to her lips.

"Fuck me, Bree," I groan as we pull onto Cedar

Lane. I'm rock hard and she's whispering, "I'm about to."

She's a vixen in disguise. All the years did to Bree was give her confidence and a sex appeal that's undeniable.

It's possible the alcohol has a little something to do with it too. Her bottom lip is wine stained and I notice as she licks her bottom lip just slightly before her teeth tug at it. I wish my teeth were doing the tugging and nipping and her lips were on mine.

"You're not too drunk are you?" I ask her, knowing damn well we sat there drinking and talking for hours.

"If you don't take me inside right now Bennet Thompson I will never forgive you," she tells me with a broad smile as she shakes her head no to my question.

"Thank fuck," I breathe out and she lets out a laugh that's still heard when I close my truck door and run around the truck to hers.

I help her out, holding her door open and attempting to contain myself but little miss Bree sidles up to me. Her hand in mine, her body against mine and a warmth and a need that's addictive.

It's heaven like I've never known.

The street lights down Cedar Lane give plenty of light as she unlocks the door and lets me in. All the while I lean down and kiss her neck, letting my hands linger on her hips as she fiddles with the keys.

Her soft hums of delight and little touches are inviting and stir a desire to please her like I've never known. Vaguely I'm all too aware that tonight needs to be damn good for her if I ever want to see her again.

The second her door opens her hands are on the lapels of my shirt, tugging me in and the grin grows on my face. My head swings with the dizziness of a night of drinking combined with the years worth of temptation toying with me. Aubrey kisses me like she always has. Like it's natural and easy. I fucking love it.

I kick her door shut as she tosses the keys carelessly on the foyer table. The stairs are a challenge so I lead her to the living room.

With our hands all over each other, neither of us has the ability to search for a light switch. Not that we need one. The bay window curtains are open, and the light from the moon streams in beautifully. The dim light cradles her gorgeous face and as she unzips her dress and lets it fall I'm in awe. She's so fucking confident. If we'd gone after what we wanted years ago, there's no telling how different life would be.

As her hands slip up my shirt I take a step back and then another, praying the back of my knees hit the sofa.

She busies herself with my zipper and all the while I drink her in. The gorgeous lace lingerie hugs her curves perfectly. I make an effort to try to remember how beautiful she looks right now. The lace. The light. The desire in her hooded eyes. She's fucking breathtaking.

As my pants fall to the floor, I slip my fingers between the lace and her warmth, finding her clit and strumming. Her lips part and our kiss breaks as she moans. Even her hands still. I smirk down at her as pleasure overwhelms her.

"That's it, isn't it?" I question in a breathy tone, helping her fall beneath me to the sofa. Her back arches and she spreads her legs for me. Fucking beautiful.

I have to kick my boxers off, multitasking as I bring her to the edge of her first orgasm. Her small hand moves to mine, as if to stop me as the sensation gets too intense.

"Bennet," she mewls and I take that moment to

slip two fingers inside of her as I kiss the curve of her neck. Her back arches and her bottom lip drops down as she sucks in a breath.

"Come for me," I tell her and as if on command her pussy spasms on my fingers. She's so fucking tight.

Her toes curl and it takes everything in me to remove myself from her, just to stroke my dick once and line up my cock at her entrance. With one hand bracing me, I tower over her and bend down to kiss her as I enter her in one swift stroke.

Her cry of pleasure is fucking everything as I pound into her with a reckless need. She's tight and slick and warm. Everything that I could ever want and more.

Her arms wrap around my back to keep her grounded and her nails scratch lightly at my back as I fuck her with a desperate need. I'm not gentle. Every thrust is brutal and deep.

"Bennet," she cries out my name and I fucking love it.

She takes it like a good girl.

As my pleasure builds I reach between us and give her clit more attention, loving the soft sounds she makes. Before I'm ready, she comes again.

The feel of her cunt milking me is unreal. I groan

in the crook of her neck, loving every second of it as she calls out my name.

I don't stop, riding through her orgasm until I find my own release.

Holy shit. I'm as breathless as she is when we come down from the highest high.

I pepper her with kisses once I come to my senses. I can't believe that just happened. She cradles herself into me as I lay down against the back of the sofa.

Naked, sated and living a dream I didn't dare have.

As our breathing calms and time passes it's quiet. Almost like both of us are realizing there's no going back now.

I wonder if I should head out or cuddle up with her longer. I don't know what exactly she expects or what she wants.

"We can't sleep down here. Come upstairs with me?" she asks and I love how it's more of a statement than a question.

"Lead the way Bree baby," I tell her and kiss just beneath the shell of her ear, loving how it makes her shiver. Our eyes lock a second too long and I swear I see something there. Something that makes me realize just how fast my heart is beating.

chapter Five

Bree

NEVER HAVE I EVER.

I feel like I'm back in grade school with the way my friends are looking at me. Wide eyed and in disbelief. Thankfully Marlena cracks the largest smile.

"You're kidding," Lauren says but the smile she dons is one of pride.

"On the first night?" Gemma questions all the while she sports a wine stained grin.

And it's only lunch time. The booze has been flowing in celebration of me having an actual date. "You don't waste any time," Gemma snickers behind her drink.

"Well alright then," Lauren states and lifts her chardonnay in a mock toast.

The blush is incredibly hot at my collar even though I'm wearing a simple silk tank and slacks. I might be having a cocktail with lunch because it's Friday but I have work after this.

"So... are you happy you took him up on his offer for a date? I'm going to guess yes?" Lauren presses.

"Incredibly," I admit. It's almost a dream but far too easy. I keep waiting for the other shoe to drop.

"So are you guys a thing?" Marlena asks, running her fingers through her long brunette hair. Her brow arches and I don't know what to say.

"I have no idea," I tell her. I don't admit just how nervous that question makes me. I'm falling way too fast. "Last night was perfect but like... we didn't talk about it."

As I shift in my seat trying to shake off the nerves, I'm reminded of the soreness between my legs. Cue the blush to come back full force. Bennet didn't hold back last night and I freaking loved it.

"So how did it end this morning?" Gemma asks, her questioning eyes on me. As if she can figure out if we're a thing or not. And heck, maybe she can? I'm not sure. I haven't been on the dating scene in forever. She has though.

"With morning breath," I reluctantly admit, making Lauren's eyes go wide. "Not that I think he smelled it or anything but he woke me up like this," I show them by gently shaking Gemma's arm, "to tell me he had to slip out and go to work."

"How early?" Marlena asks questioningly. She even has a brow arched.

"Just before six." I add to give credibility to him, "he said there was a work emergency and he was needed."

Marlena and Lauren share a look but Gemma pipes up, "I bet Joe needed help with a tow."

I shrug, sipping on the sweet tea and not liking how my stomach turns at the thought of him leaving so early.

"So no morning sex?" Lauren asks the important question as the waiter walks by. Marlena snickers and I pretend not to notice the look from the poor guy who pretends he didn't hear anything. The diner on the corner boasts a beautiful quiet booth in the back. With shrubbery on the corner of mainstreet. We are sheltered away with paper napkins and fold out chairs.

"No morning sex," I admit before lifting my sweet tea to my lips and taking a gulp.

The girls laugh and I laugh along with them. "I wish we would have though. I'm absolutely up for round two."

"Girl!" Marlena calls out and the waiter looks back our way causing laughter amongst the group. We're not typically rowdy but today is a day for celebration if I do say so myself.

"So it was good?" Lauren states the question with a thinly veiled smile

"It was good," I admit and cover my face. I can't stop smiling. Bennet was everything I remembered and more. Sweet and charming, but friendly and comical. All the while holding a sex appeal that makes me want for nothing short of him.

"It was amazing," I add, dreamily.

The girls all make their comments but Gemma asks the tough questions. "How long has it been?"

"Over a year and I don't want to even think about that mistake," I answer and cling to my sweet tea.

"Has he text you yet?"

never got over *you*

"No," I answer and take a gulp. That nervousness creeps back up. It was amazing for me. But for him? I have no idea. "He just left a few hours ago," I tell them as if they can't count from six to twelve and then check my phone again. Nothing from him.

A cold sweep flows through me.

"Well why don't you text him?" Gemma suggests and the other girls nod.

"Is that not too forward?" I ask and Marlena shrugs, she's been married for seemingly forever.

"It's the 2000s babe, women take the lead now," Lauren says and the table laughs again. Maybe I will call him, I think as I look into my tea and then back to my phone, wishing he would tell me he enjoyed last night as much as I did.

chapter Six

Bennet

For as long as I can remember I've had a fascination with cars... and Bree Peters.

"You're moving slow," Joe calls out. "Come on man, drink too much last night?" he questions and I can tell from the look on his face he knows I was out last night.

And I'm sure he knows I was out with Bree too.

"Had a little to drink last night, is all," I tell him. I don't tell him the part where I didn't sleep much.

Too busy enjoying all those curves and small kisses from the girl of my dreams.

He starts to laugh and then groans. "Hand me that advil will you?" He gestures to the bench and I grab the bottle for him.

It's been a long hard day. Joe needs another person, maybe a few more people, to do all that the shop takes on. I take a moment to wipe down my hands with the blue rag. We've been going non stop since this morning and all I can wonder in every small moment is whether or not Bree messaged me. Or whether I should text her.

"You need one?" he asks me as he screws the lid on and tosses me the bottle of pills. My brow creases as I tell him no, I'm fine.

"I was thinking from the workout you got last night?" he guesses and the shock followed by a wide grin I try to hide most certainly gives it away.

Heat flows up the back of my neck as I turn my back to him to keep him from seeing.

"Word in the small town is that you hooked up with Aubrey last night. You two really hit it off didn't you?" he asks and the clang of a wrench in his hand lets me know he plans on talking while we work.

Fucking hell; small town's never change do they?

"Maybe we did. It's none of anyone's business," I tell him in an attempt to be a gentleman to Bree. I have no idea if she cares if anyone in this town is talking about her or not. I sure as hell don't.

I crouch down as he tells me to hand him the lug nuts one by one as he points with his wrench. Peering up at the clock I count the hours since I left Bree.

Time is ticking by too fast and just thinking about her and what she's thinking has my gut churning. Instinctively I look towards the bench where my coat is hung over the back of the chair and my phone snugly in a pocket.

"Is it a thing or just a fling?" Joe asks and I don't know the answer.

As my nerves tick inside of me I stare back at my lifelong friend and ask him sarcastically, "Are you a poet?"

He just laughs and blows me off. He rubs his cheek with the back of his hand, smearing oil there and I let out a laugh.

"I don't know what it is," I answer him half heartedly as I stand up and stretch before handing him the other lug nut. "I just like the woman and as far as I can tell, she likes me too."

Just saying that out loud does something to me.

It's almost like a dream, how the spark was still there and the tension crackled like that. How the conversation flowed and we never missed a beat.

"When are you seeing her again?" he asks and I clear my throat.

Shifting my weight back and forth I debate on asking him, but decide just to go for it. "Is it too soon to ask her out tonight?"

"Only if you want her to think she's got you hook, line and sinker," he answers flatly, like he's not really paying attention anymore. I nod although he can't see me.

I don't tell him, but I think I'm alright with that. I'm absolutely fine with her knowing she's got me however she wants me.

I'm head over heels for her and I don't care who knows. Funny how time changes things like that. Years ago, I'd have been terrified. I'd have cared what everyone else thought. Now all I can wonder what Aubrey Peters thinks of us. No one else matters.

chapter Seven

Aubrey

HIS SMILE IS THE SAME AS WHEN I FIRST saw him in the garage, but the way he easily lays his hand on my thigh is different. Like he knows that I want him to and I want everything just like he does. And I freaking love it.

"Two nights in a row?" I joke with him as we sit back on the bench at the fire pit.

Mickey's is perfect for tonight. Cold beer, a bonfire, and good music.

"What can I say? I like what I like," Bennet says and holds my gaze as he takes a swig of beer. Mickey's is a fun spot, easy going with Italian fare and a younger crowd. It's newer to this town and judging by how busy it is, it's going well.

"It's different," Bennet says in reference to the bar and I agree, "A bit different from Carole's Coffee House that's for sure."

"They had the best donuts," I comment and Bennet agrees. "Remember when we used them as goals for paper footballs and we got in trouble?" he asks and I let out a small laugh. We were just kids, and Carole was not having it.

She retired and moved away, leaving this place empty for a good year after we graduated.

"She told my mom," I confess to him remembering how embarrassed she was that I would get in trouble at the Coffee House of all places.

"I bet your mom thought I was the problem."

"Never," I shut that thought down fast. "She always liked you," I tell him and he lets a small smile slip on his lips before taking a swig.

"I wish I'd known that," he comments but it's quickly overshadowed.

The music flows louder as the waiter opens the

never got over *you*

door, the tray in hand. As the door closes, the music from inside dims. The waiter, Tanner, is the owner's son and looks just like him. For a moment I think the tray is ours, but he takes it to the other side of the back patio. There are only two couples outside, since it's a bit colder tonight. I like the privacy though and the throw blanket they have on the benches helps with the chill.

"I remember when Mickey opened the place," I tell Bennet. "It was a good time. Lauren got drunk off her butt and Derek had to scurry her away."

He laughs at the imagery and then says, "Sorry I missed it."

I almost ask him if he's leaving again, but I bite my tongue and take another drink.

"Yours should be right out," Tanner tells us, "Another round?" he asks and both Bennet and I answer yes.

We share a look and I blush before turning my attention back to the beer in my hand.

A car drives by and the lights shine onto the shrubbery and trees. With the soft din of music and the beautiful night sky, it's picture perfect out here. But all I can focus on is that I have no idea if we're just friends who took it a little too far once, or if Bennet wants what I want.

Tanner comes around before I can speak up. The glass bottles tapping on the glass table top of the outdoor table.

We say our thanks and he heads off, hopefully to get our pizza. A gust of wind blows by and I'm surprised by how chilly it is. And regretful that I didn't grab a cardigan to throw over my tank top.

He might think he's sly, but I know exactly what Bennet is doing as he extends his arm around and his thumb finds my shoulder.

"It's a bit colder, if you wanted," he says and nods his head to the left, inviting me to scoot closer.

A grab the throw blanket and scoot closer to him, laying it over my lap and enjoying his warmth. His scent. Everything about him.

I mold my body to his and those questions come back.

"So I have a question to ask…"

I peer up at him, the bottle at my lips, "And what's that?"

"You think you might want to be my girlfriend?"

"Girlfriend?" I question, staring into his pale blue eyes through my thick lashes.

"Whatever you want to call it. Just us… a thing? I'm not picky about titles," he tells me and my smile grows wider. "I know it's only been two dates and I've been gone a long time, but I want to keep seeing you. As long as you do, I'd like to pick you up and take you out and spend the night with you."

A warmth settles in my chest and I notice how he picks at the label on his bottle. "You nervous?" I ask him.

His smile widens and I have to laugh.

"Is that a yes?" he questions and I laugh with him.

"I like it when you're nervous."

"You are such a tease, Bree," he responds, leaning back and raking his hand through his hair like it's actually making him nervous.

I lean over and kiss his cheek before saying, "Yes. I would love to be your girlfriend or whatever you want to call it."

"Good," he says before leaning down and deepening the kiss.

The door to the restaurant opens but I don't care to look. Nothing is getting in the way of me and Bennet and this kiss in this moment.

I'm holding onto it forever. I'll never forget it.

chapter Eight

Bennet

EVERY NIGHT FOR TWO WEEKS I'VE KISSED her good night.

More than half of the days, I've kissed her good morning.

Everyone knows we're a couple and I fucking love it.

I never knew life could be this damn good. If I'd known, I never would have left. But fate has a funny way of pulling two people apart so they know just how perfect they are together.

I know the curve of her waist. I know the way she loves to lay on her right side at night and how perfectly her ass cradles into me. And I know almost every little thing about her.

We share secrets like we did when we were kids and as the night gets long I wonder if I should confess to her that before I left I wanted to make a deal with her. That if we were both single in ten years, we'd date each other. Back then, I considered making it marriage. I never did ask her though and I'm scared to tell her how much I thought of her back then. I don't want to ruin this.

What's between Aubrey and I is fucking perfect. If I could sit in this bar in this small town every night, kiss her to sleep and kiss her in the morning for as long as I live, I'll be a happy man.

The thoughts escape me as she pushes her glass away and distracts me from the game, nudging her nose against mine and kissing me. I fucking love how she goes for it. How nothing stops her from letting me know she wants me.

Her lips mold to mine easily in the back of the bar. It's mostly empty, the corner dimly lit. Someone in this small town might be watching. They might say something and honestly I hope they do. Tell this town I'm madly in love with her. That I came back here after years of wondering what could have been. They can also gossip about how I can't keep my hands off of her. Let them.

I want the world to know I love Aubrey Peters and I always have.

She lets out the softest most tempting feminine sound as she pulls away. A mix between a satisfied hum and a moan.

I almost tell her I love her. I almost say it out loud but that would be crazy, wouldn't it?

"I don't know if I can have another round," she says into the glass after downing the last bit of liquid and leaving behind only a few slivers of ice.

"Light weight," I tease her and then glance at the clock. It's almost midnight.

She chuckles sweet and low before batting my shoulder and getting more comfortable in the booth. Her hands on my body, even if it is just playful... *fuck me.*

My cock's already hard. The leather of the booth groans as she gets closer to me and tilts her chin up to kiss me. I'm quick to put my beer down and eager for her touch.

Her lips are sweet and the hint of citrus is divine. The way she arches her back though... I know exactly what that means.

"Maybe we should get out of here," I murmur against her lips when the kiss gets hotter.

"Maybe you should move in with me," she comments like it's nothing. "Or at least a box of clothes or something," she adds as if to minimize what she's just suggested. My brow arches and I stare down at this beautiful woman wondering if she's feeling everything I've been feeling. Wondering if she's loved me as long as I've loved her.

"I couldn't do that to you," I tell her although to be frank, I'd go anywhere as long as she's there. I'm addicted to kissing her, in love with loving her... I'm a goner and there's no coming back from loving her. "Besides what would your family say?"

"You're... ridiculous Bennet Thompson," she whispers at my lips and I lean forward just slightly to kiss her one more time. "And they'd probably be grateful I'm dating someone but especially happy that it's you."

I don't expect that answer and I don't know what

to think of it other than to be thankful for the relief it gives me.

I almost say it as I stare deep into her eyes… I almost tell her I love her, but we can wait one more night. After all, I want her forever and ever. One night isn't going to change that.

Epilogue

Aubrey

It's ridiculous ... but I keep clicking. As if it has all the answers and I can truly trust the yes/no dial. I spin it, with tears in my eyes and the plastic arrow sits between the yes and the no. The bottle of wine is empty and the dark green is only lit from the moonlight that shines through the kitchen window.

Perched on the chair I spin it again, no question

in mind this time and it sits perfectly between the black and white. The yes and the no.

Swallowing thickly I whisper the question, a safer one this time, "Was it love at first sight?"

Yes.

My vision turns blurry as I force myself to look away. My phone still shows a list of messages from my friends. I can't respond though, all I can do tonight is think of him and the dreams I've been having.

They're so vivid as if I've actually been with him. As if he's still here in some way.

"Will I see him again?" I can't help but ask and with the answer, my heart shatters all over again.

Yes.

It's only a toy. It's some piece to a board game or something that I happened to find under the sofa. It's stupid but drunkenly I believe it. It's been long enough that the police should know where he is. Search and rescue should have turned up something… anything

"Will I love someone else in this lifetime?" I question and immediately feel guilty. The pain of losing him is unbearable; the pain of saying goodbye is just as awful. I know he's the only man I've ever loved.

No.

I reach for the wine glass only to find it empty.

never got over *you*

The slight push of the stool legs against the kitchen floor is the only sound in the empty house.

I swipe away the messages asking me if I'm alright and instead stare at the wallpaper on my phone. I stare at him and know he is my soulmate. There will never be anyone else for me.

Wiping under my eyes I stare up at the ceiling and try to hold it together. I still have hope and that's what hurts the most. Hope is a long way of saying goodbye.

"Is he still alive?" I ask with my head back, aimlessly watching the ceiling fan turn. Without looking I hit the dial and wait.

They say I need to let him go. They say he's gone. But I know deep in my soul he's still alive. My gaze drops and the little arrow sits on the yes.

I can barely see it through the tears and just as I break down, falling into the same pain I've slept with the last two months, my phone rings.

This is not the end...
The *Fall in Love Again* series will feature Bennet and Bree falling in love on the small fictional street of Cedar Lane over and over again while the real world has had other plans for them. Because love is endless and this is what forever means. In any and every life, their love was meant to be. And there's so much to tell in the dreams where they get to meet again for the first time every night.

There is more to come from the
Fall in Love Again series.

about the *Author*

Thank you so much for reading my romances. I'm just a stay at home mom and avid reader turned author and I couldn't be happier.

I hope you love my books as much as I do!

More by Willow Winters
www.WillowWintersWrites.com/books

Made in the USA
Middletown, DE
07 January 2024